Dinosaur
Fossils

Dr. Alvin Granowsky

RSVP
RAINTREE
STECK-VAUGHN
PUBLISHERS
The Steck-Vaughn Company
Austin, Texas

Illustrations by
Lee Herring

We have learned all that we know about dinosaurs from their fossils.
A fossil is what is left of a plant or an animal that lived long ago.

Fossils can be leaves, shells,
eggs, or skeletons.
Some fossils are hardened tracks or footprints
left by a moving animal.

When a plant or animal dies,
it can become covered with mud or sand.

As time goes by, the plant or animal becomes covered by many layers of mud and sand. After thousands of years, the bottom layers harden into rock.

The dead plant or animal also hardens into rock.
This is how fossils are formed.

Any plant or animal can become a fossil.
Animal fossils are usually the hard parts
of the body such as teeth, bones, or shells.

Sometimes an animal's whole body is frozen
in ice or covered very quickly with river mud.
Then scientists can study the skin
and other soft parts of an animal's body.

Sometimes fossils are found by chance.
Fossils may be uncovered
by workers digging a well or roadway.

Most often, scientists who study fossils
have to spend a long time looking for them.
These scientists are called paleontologists.

Fossils found in soft ground
are the easiest ones to collect.
Paleontologists can dig them out
with a shovel or by hand.

Fossils have to be loosened slowly from rocks.
Scientists use chisels, hammers, or picks
to remove the fossils.
They work carefully to protect the fossils.

Then the hardest work begins.
Most fossils are found in pieces.
The bones are like the pieces of a puzzle.
Putting the bones together is difficult
when some of the pieces are missing.

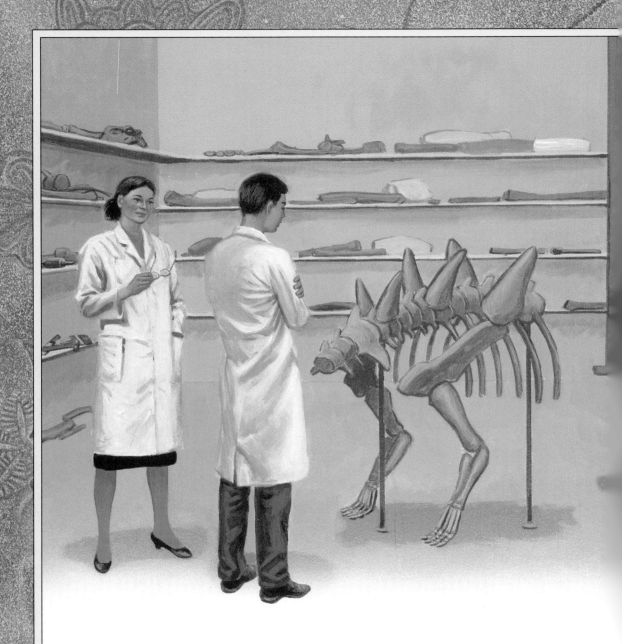

What if some of the fossil pieces don't belong?
That often happens when the fossils
of many animals are found in the same place.

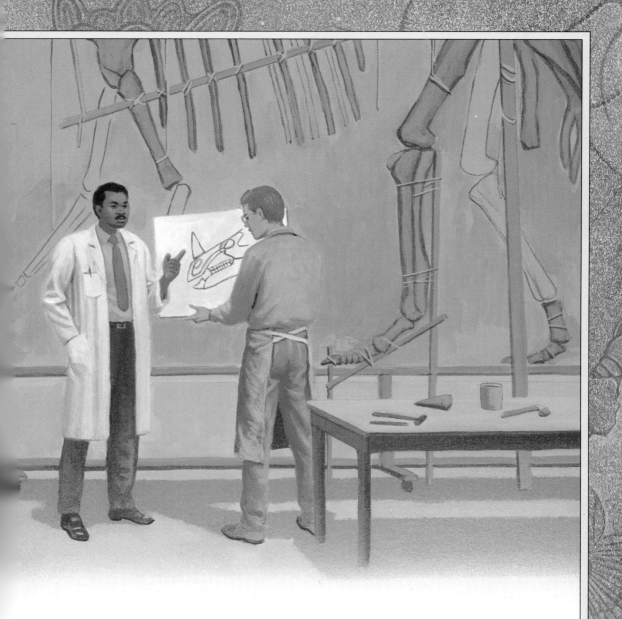

Sometimes scientists make mistakes
when they work with fossils.
At one time, they thought the thumb-claw
of an Iguanodon was a horn on its nose.

15

But scientists learn from their mistakes.
They work until they find the right way
to put the bones together.
The skeletons are placed in museums
so that everyone can learn about dinosaurs.

16

Scientists must learn about dinosaurs from fossils
because dinosaurs are extinct.
When scientists say that dinosaurs are extinct
they mean that dinosaurs are not alive today.

For a long time, we didn't know
that dinosaurs had ever lived.

Then dinosaur fossils were found.
Scientists learned that dinosaurs
had once lived all over Earth.

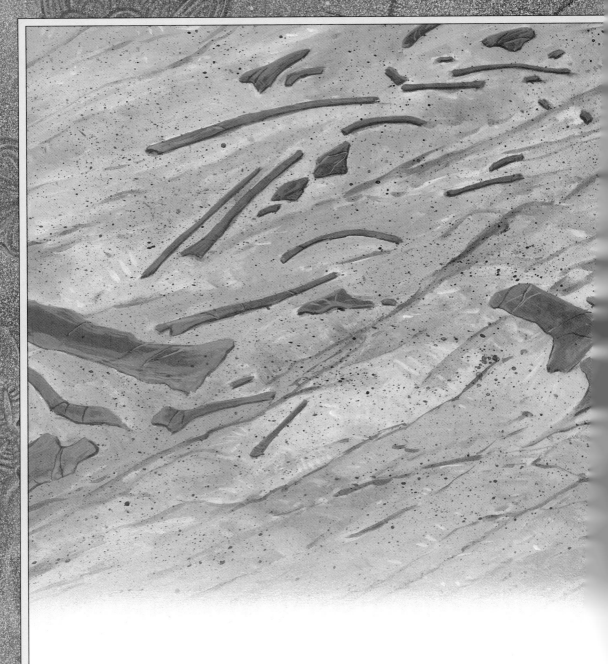

When the first dinosaur fossils were found,
people wondered, "What kind of bone is this?"

People saw how big the bones were.
They asked, "Could these be the bones
of an elephant?"

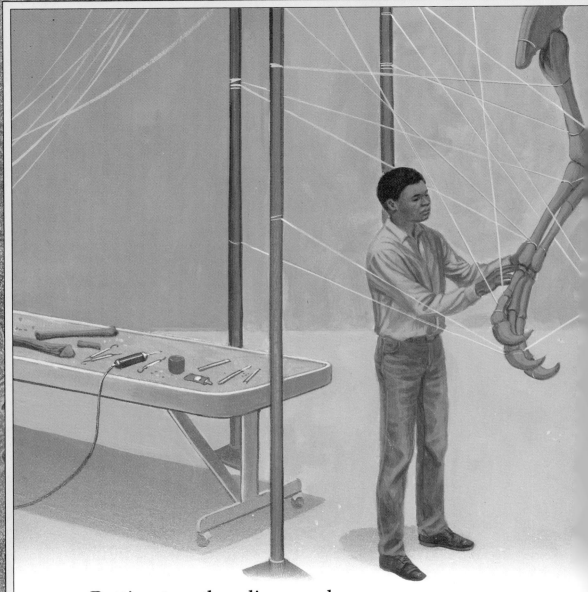

Putting together dinosaur bones
was slow work.
Scientists tried putting the bones together
in different ways.

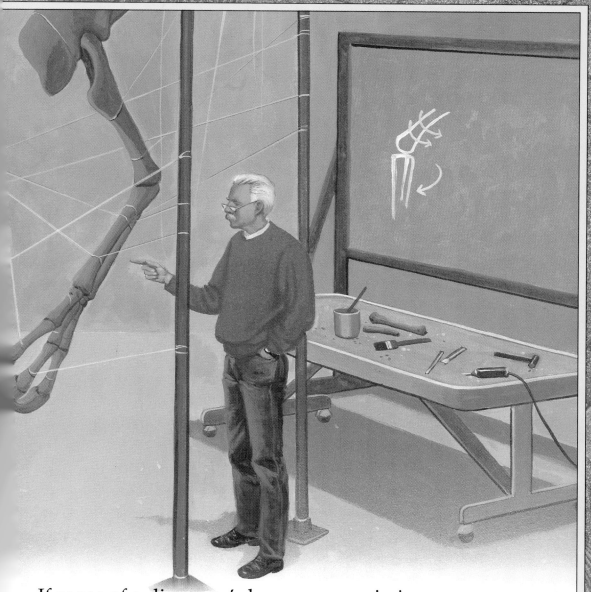

If some of a dinosaur's bones were missing,
the job was even slower.
Sometimes scientists had to guess
what the missing parts looked like.

At one time, scientists thought they had discovered
a new dinosaur called a Polacanthus.
Scientists had only part of the skeleton, but they
tried to imagine what a Polacanthus looked like.
They thought that the Polacanthus
had a small head and spikes along its back.

But later, scientists found other bones
that belonged to the same skeleton.
With the new bones, scientists could see
that the skeleton was from a Hylaeosaurus.

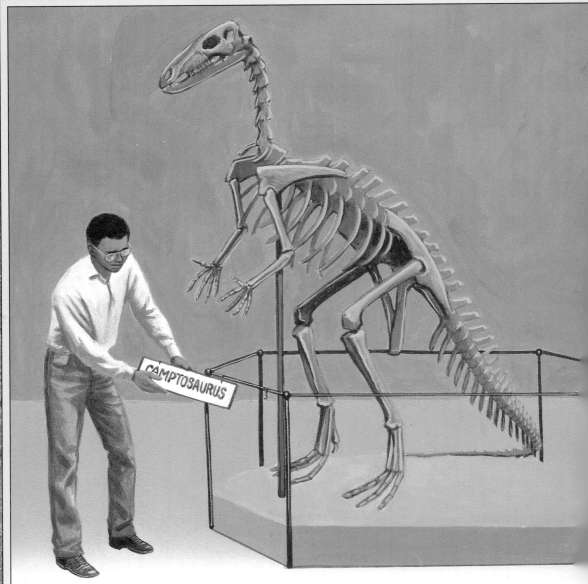

Sometimes scientists find many dinosaur bones in one place.
In Wyoming, scientists discovered several complete skeletons of Camptosaurus dinosaurs.

That made it easier to describe a Camptosaurus.
After studying the skeletons, scientists decided
that the Camptosaurus grew as long as 23 feet.

Tyrannosaurus

Stenonychosaurus

Saltasaurus

NORTH AMERICA

SOUTH AMERICA

ANTARCTICA

Dinosaur fossils have been found in many places around the world.

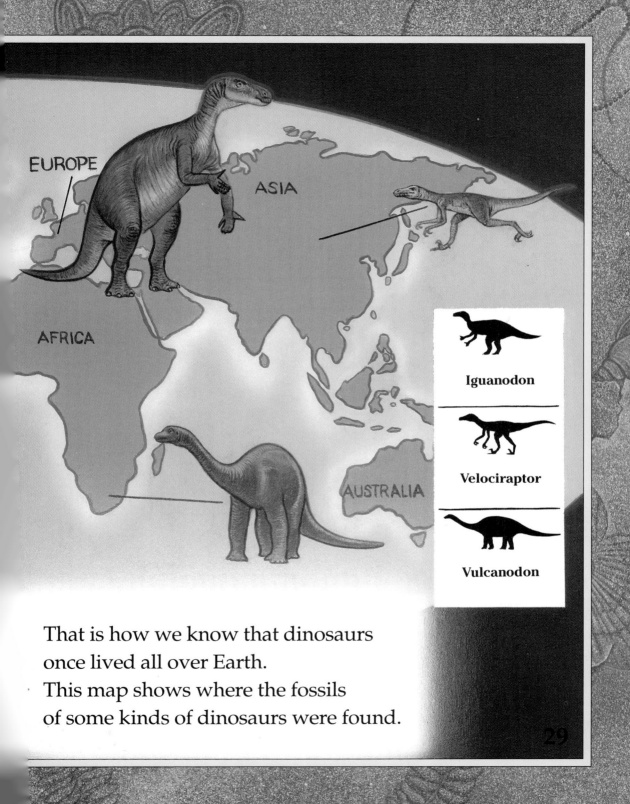

EUROPE

ASIA

AFRICA

AUSTRALIA

Iguanodon

Velociraptor

Vulcanodon

That is how we know that dinosaurs
once lived all over Earth.
This map shows where the fossils
of some kinds of dinosaurs were found.

29

Dinosaur bones show us that there were dinosaurs of all shapes and sizes.
The skeletons scientists put together help us see how different each kind of dinosaur was.

The skeleton of a Tyrannosaurus Rex stands on
two legs and has big, sharp teeth.
The skeleton of an Apatosaurus shows
its long, thin neck and tail.

New fossils are still being found today.
Someday you could be a scientist
and put together a dinosaur skeleton.

Look for these animals in
Dinosaur Fossils

Ankylosaurus
(an KY luh SAWR uhs)
19

Iguanodon
(ih GWAHN uh dahn)
15, **29**

Stenonychosaurus
(sten oh nike uh SAWR uhs)
28

Apatosaurus
(a pat uh SAWR uhs)
31, 31

Maiasaura
(my uh SAWR uh)
8

Triceratops
(try SEHR uh tahps)
19, **30**

Brachiosaurus
(brak ee uh SAWR uhs)
17

Ornitholestes
(or nith oh LESS teez)
17

Tyrannosaurus
(tih ran uh SAWR uhs)
4, 5, 18, 28, 30, 31

Camptosaurus
(kamp tuh SAWR uhs)
16, 26-27, **26-27**

Saltasaurus
(sahl tuh SAWR uhs)
28

Velociraptor
(vuh lahs uh RAP tawr)
29

Hylaeosaurus
(hy lee uh SAWR uhs)
25, 25

Stegosaurus
(stehg uh SAWR uhs)
17, **32**

Vulcanodon
(vul KAN oh don)
29

Boldface type indicates that the animal appears in an illustration.

Acknowledgments
Design and Production: Design Five, N.Y.
Illustrations: Lee Herring
Line Art: John Harrison

Staff Credits
Executive Editor: Elizabeth Strauss
Project Editor: Becky Ward
Project Manager: Sharon Golden

Library of Congress Cataloging-in-Publication Data

Granowsky, Alvin, 1936–
    Dinosaur fossils / written by Alvin Granowsky: illustrated by Lee Herring.
      p. cm.—(World of dinosaurs)
    Summary: Explains the significance of dinosaur fossils and the work of
paleontologists.
    ISBN 0-8114-3253-X
    1. Dinosaurs—Juvenile literature. 2. Fossils—Juvenile literature.
3. Paleontologists—Juvenile literature. [1. Dinosaurs. 2. Fossils. 3. Paleontology.]
I. Herring, Lee, ill. II. Title. III. Series.
QE862.D5G732   1992
567.9'1—dc20   91-23407
                                                          CIP AC

2 3 4 5 6 7 8 9 LB 96 95 94 93